Moritz Petz was born in Hamburg, Germany. Upon completion of his studies, he traveled through Italy, Denmark, and Sweden, working a variety of jobs before returning to study history and German. His interests include street- and puppet-theater, chess, music, and writing. Today he works as a freelance author and lives on Lake Constance in Germany.

Amélie Jackowski was born in Toulon, France. She studied at the Higher School of Decorative Arts in Strasbourg and at the University of Provence in France. She has published many children's books. Her work has been exhibited at numerous group shows, including the Bologna Children's Book Fair in Italy. She lives in France and works as a freelance illustrator.

Copyright © 2015 by NordSüd Verlag AG, CH-8005 Zürich, Switzerland.
First published in Switzerland under the title *Der Dachs hat heute einfach Pech*.
English translation copyright © 2015 by NorthSouth Book, Inc., New York 10016.
Translated by David Henry Wilson.

This edition published in the United States, Great Britain, Canada, Australia, and New Zealand in 2015 by NorthSouth Books, Inc., an imprint of NordSüd Verlag AG, CH-8005 Zürich, Switzerland.

Distributed in the United States by NorthSouth Books, Inc., New York 10016.
Library of Congress Cataloging-in-Publication Data is available.
ISBN: 978-0-7358-4209-0
Printed in Germany by Grafisches Centrum Cuno GmbH & Co. KG, Calbe, January 2015.
1 3 5 7 9 · 10 8 6 4 2
www.northsouth.com

FSC
www.fsc.org
MIX
Paper from
responsible sources
FSC® C043106

THE DAY EVERYTHING WENT WRONG

by **Moritz Petz**

illustrated by **Amélie Jackowski**

North
South

*T*oday I'll give myself a real treat, thought Badger. *I'll only do things I enjoy doing!*

But when he got out of bed, he knocked over his bedside lamp. Luckily, it didn't break.

That's all right, thought Badger.

Badger was in the best of moods as he sat down at the breakfast table. But unfortunately, he didn't watch what he was doing, and his cup fell on the floor and broke.

Oh, what a shame! thought Badger. *That was my favorite cup!*

After breakfast, Badger decided to draw a nice picture.
But he couldn't find his colored pencils anywhere.

"What's gone wrong?" cried Badger. "Today was going
to be such a treat! Oh well, I'll go outside in the yard. My
yard is the loveliest place. And it's always fun."

Badger played around outside, until he tripped over his shovel and accidentally knocked over the wheelbarrow.

I've had enough of this, thought Badger. This is turning out to be a really rotten day! Hmm, I'll go see my friends. Here at home, only bad things are happening to me.

First Badger went to see Raccoon. He
tried to tell him what a miserable day he'd
been having, but Raccoon didn't even listen.

Instead, Raccoon complained, "My clothesline
broke, and today is my washing day!"

"Oh, we can fix that," said Badger reassuringly.
Then he tied a knot in Raccoon's clothesline and
hung it up again.

Raccoon was able to get on with his work.

Next Badger visited Stag, but he wasn't happy either.

"I was going to play with my ball today," Stag moaned, "but I can't find it! And I've looked everywhere!"

Badger sighed. He helped Stag search for the ball, and found it hidden under a bush.

Then Badger went to see the rest of his friends, but it turned out that all of them were having a thoroughly miserable day.

Squirrel had a nasty scratch, so Badger helped him put a bandage on it. Rabbit's fishing line was tangled, so Badger helped to straighten it out. Fox's front door was blocked, so Badger shoveled away the earth. And Mouse simply couldn't manage to bake a cake by herself no matter how hard she tried.

For some reason, everything is going wrong today, thought Badger as he walked down to the stream. *At least I was able to help my friends. That's some consolation.*

But a minute later, Badger slipped, slid, and fell into the water. "This is really too much!" groaned Badger. "What a horrible day! I'm going home and straight to bed. Then nothing else can happen to me."

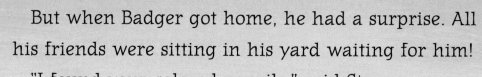

But when Badger got home, he had a surprise. All
his friends were sitting in his yard waiting for him!
"I found your colored pencils," said Stag.
"I glued your cup together," said Squirrel.
"We picked up your tools," said Fox and Rabbit.
"I brought a towel so you can dry off," said Raccoon.
"And I brought you a cake," squeaked Mouse.

When Badger dried himself, he and his friends ate the delicious cake.

Then they played games: Who was best at slipping, sliding, and falling. Who could say "What a horrible day!" most miserably. And who could knock over his cup most clumsily.

When at last Badger was alone again and was about to snuggle up in his cozy bed, his pillow almost fell to the floor, but he was just able to catch it.

"What a bad . . ." Badger sighed, but then he couldn't help laughing.

"What a . . . badger of a day!" he said.

He reached out to turn off the light, but he accidentally knocked the lamp. It wiggled and waggled, quivered and shivered . . . but it didn't fall down.

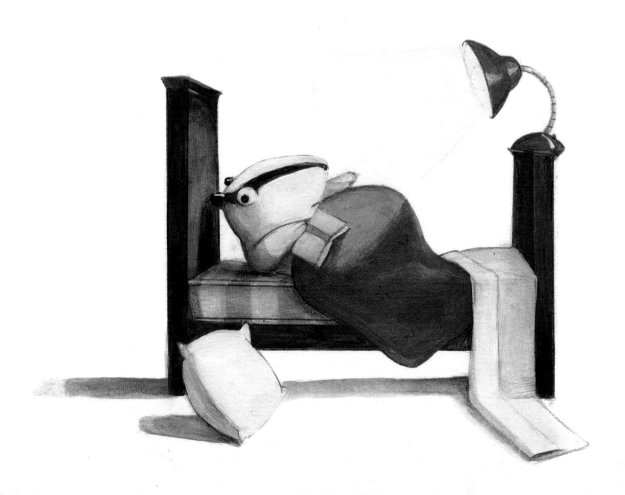